Laughing All the Way

George Shannon

Illustrated by Meg McLean

Houghton Mifflin Company
Boston   1992

To Nate and Anna Rice
—G.S.

To Leslie and Tucker,
for paving the way.
—M.M.

Text copyright © 1992 by George Shannon
Illustrations copyright © 1992 by Meg McLean

Library of Congress Cataloging-in-Publication Data

Shannon, George.
  Laughing all the way / George Shannon ; illustrated by Meg McLean.
    p.   cm.
  Summary: Bear catches Duck and tries to pluck out all his
feathers, but Duck outsmarts him.
  ISBN 0-395-62473-8
  [1. Ducks—Fiction. 2. Bears—Fiction.]   I. McLean, Meg, ill.
II. Title.
PZ7.S5287Lau 1992   91-41135
[E]—dc20   CIP
            AC

Printed in the United States of America

WOZ 10 9 8 7 6 5 4 3 2 1

Duck woke up late, and everything after that went from wrong to worse.

He had a crick in his neck,

he tripped on a stone,

and when he got to the river
all his friends were gone.

"Fiddle figs!" grumbled Duck.

"It's the worst-ever worst day of all my life."

A grumpy goose was swimming
in Duck's favorite spot,

a bug bit his tail, and when
he took a bite of grass
he bit a fat prickle burr.

"Fiddle figs!" fussed Duck. "It's the worst-ever worst day of all my life." He walked on, grumbling and wagging his head.

"NOTHING'S going right.
I might as well WALK back
home to bed.

If I tried to fly now
I'd probably hit a tree!
It's the worst-ever
worst day
of all my life."

13

Duck turned to go home, but his day got worse.

Bear grabbed him tight.

"One!

I'm plucking all your feathers for
a soft winter bed. Two!"

19

"Stelp! Stelp!" cried Duck.
"Hop. Get me low!"

"Do WHAT?" said Bear as he laughed a big laugh.
"You're not making sense."

"Met me toe . . . let me GO!" Duck was so mad at the
thought of getting caught and being plucked that his tongue
was tangling up and making things even worse.
"Figgle fids! NOTHING'S rowing GIGHT."

"I hope," laughed Bear, shaking his head, "that all your feathers are as soft as your brain!"

"I mean going RIGHT!" yelled Duck. "It's the durst-ever lurst day of ALL my fife."

Bear was laughing so hard his whole body shook, including his paws, which tickled Duck's sides.

"TON'T DICKLE!" Duck giggled. He was even madder now and trying not to laugh. But the madder Duck got the more he tangled words. The more he tangled words the more Bear laughed.

25

The more Bear laughed the more he shook. The more he shook the more he tickled Duck. And the more he tickled Duck the more Duck laughed, till all of a sudden Duck knew just what to do.

"Pease Blare, pease," begged Duck as he laughed, tangling up his words even worse than before. "I'll thing any do you tell dee to moo. Just don't luck my pethers!"

"PETHERS!" Bear was laughing so hard his cheeks began to ache.

"I mean puck my jethers. I mean juck by flethers. I mean PLUCK MY FEATHERS! Honest. I'll be jenny as your faws. Fenny as your baws. I mean benny as your SAWS!"

"Duck," said Bear with a giant laugh. "You're nothing but a fool! WHAT in the world—" He was laughing so hard he grabbed his shaking sides. "WHAT in the world is 'benny as your saws'?"

"NOTHING!" called Duck as he laughed, flying free.
"Nothing, like you've got nothing in your paws!"

Bear jumped and grabbed again, but Duck was safe away.

Flying high. Flying home.

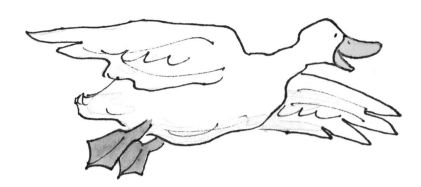

Laughing all the way.